DOLLAR STORE DANNY

and the Dangerous Dinosaur

An AudioCraft Publishing, Inc. book

Book storage and warehouses provided by *Chillermania* ©
Indian River, Michigan

Dollar $tore Danny and the Dangerous Dinosaur
Copyright © 2018 by Johnathan Rand/AudioCraft Publishing, Inc.
ISBN: 978-1-893699-40-3

Librarians/Media Specialists:
PCIP/MARC records available **free of charge** at
www.americanchillers.com

Illustrations by Michal Jacot © 2018 AudioCraft Publishing, Inc.
Cover/interior layout and graphics design by Howard Roark

Printed in USA

The
Dangerous
Dinosaur

Chapter One

It was Friday.

Every Friday, Danny went to the dollar store with his mother. He always had a lot of fun. But he always seemed to find trouble. And if Danny didn't find trouble? Well, trouble just had a way of finding him.

"Can I look at toys while you shop?" Danny asked his mother.

"Yes," his mother said. She smiled. "But stay out of trouble."

"I will," Danny said.

Danny meant it. He didn't want to get into trouble.

His mother turned and went one way. Danny went the other way.

He stopped walking when he saw plastic dinosaurs on a shelf.

"Wow," Danny whispered. He picked up one of the tiny toy dinosaurs.

"These are cool," he said. "I wish I had a real pet dinosaur of my very own."

Danny heard a loud noise. He turned to see what it was. When he saw what made the sound, he froze.

He dropped the toy dinosaur. It bounced on the floor.

Danny was very frightened. But he couldn't move. He was too scared.

At the end of the aisle, staring back at him, was a giant dinosaur!

Chapter Two

The dinosaur was very, very big.
It was taller than Danny. It was
green. It had big eyes. It had big,
sharp teeth. It looked very scary.

"Mom?" Danny called out.
He stood in one place. He was too
afraid to move.

Danny's mother did not

answer. He did not see her.

"Mom?" Danny called out again.

Still, there was no answer from his mother.

Slowly, Danny took a step back.

The big dinosaur took a step toward Danny.

Danny looked around for someone to help him. He saw no one.

The dinosaur threw his head back. He let out a loud roar. The sound was so loud that it shook

the shelves! A rubber ball fell to
the floor and bounced away.

Danny took another step back.

The dinosaur took another step forward. He roared again.

The dinosaur was standing on his hind legs. His big tail swished back and forth. Two colorful balloons attached to strings became tangled in his claws.

Danny wondered where the beast came from. He had been shopping many times with his mother. He had never before seen a live dinosaur in the dollar store.

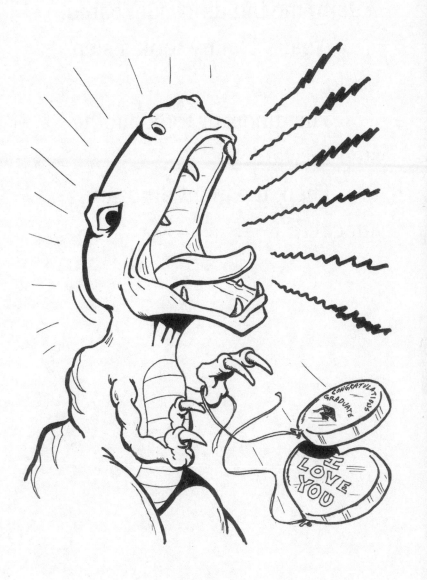

Again, the big dinosaur roared.

Again, Danny took a step back.

The dinosaur took another step forward.

Then, the giant dinosaur attacked.

Chapter Three

Danny turned and ran. He looked for his mother, but he didn't see her. He looked for someone in the dollar store who could help him. But he didn't see anyone.

Behind him was the dinosaur. He was big and green and loud and mean.

"Help!" Danny cried. He swung his arms madly as he ran. "A giant dinosaur is chasing me! Help!"

The big, green dinosaur charged. He bumped into shelves. Items crashed to the floor.

Danny ran to the end of the aisle. He looked for his mother, but he did not see her.

"Help!" he shouted again. "A giant dinosaur is trying to gobble me up!"

Danny continued to run. The dinosaur chased after him.

"Mom!" he yelled. "Mom! Help!"

But Danny was all alone.

Except for the dinosaur. The beast was coming after Danny faster than ever!

"*Raaaawwrrrr!*" the dinosaur growled.

"*Ahhhhh!*" screamed Danny. "I've got to find a place to hide!"

At that very moment, he saw a big, plastic laundry basket. It was bright blue. Danny quickly climbed inside and ducked down.

The giant green dinosaur came around the corner. He stopped. He sniffed the air.

Danny stayed inside the laundry basket. He was shaking because he was so scared.

The dinosaur sniffed the air again.

I hope he doesn't see me, Danny thought.

The dinosaur paused. Again, he sniffed the air.

He looked down.

He saw Danny in the laundry basket.

"*Raaaawwrrrr!*" the dinosaur wailed.

Danny screamed and tried to get out of the basket.

But it was too late. Danny was about to be eaten by the dinosaur!

Chapter Four

Using his long snout, the dinosaur knocked over the laundry basket.

Danny tumbled out. He rolled onto the floor.

He kept rolling.

And rolling.

And rolling.

And rolling.

Finally, he jumped to his feet and ran.

Then, he realized he was no longer in the dollar store.

All around him were large rocks and big trees. Even the floor was gone! Danny was now running on hard-packed dirt!

But even worse:

There were more dinosaurs all around!

Chapter Five

Danny was in a lot of trouble.

He spun around in a circle. He looked for a place to hide. But the giant dinosaurs were everywhere.

At his feet was the laundry basket. It was on its side.

Danny knelt down and crawled inside the laundry basket again.

He closed his eyes.

He opened them.

He was in the dollar store again!

Danny stood. He did not see the dinosaur. He looked at the laundry basket on the floor.

"Wow," he said. "I'm not going in there again."

He turned his head from side to side. The only thing he saw were items on shelves.

No dinosaur.

But he didn't see his mother, either.

Danny raced up the aisle and turned the corner. He bumped into a basket of sale items and almost knocked it over. He stopped.

"Mom?" he called out.

There was no answer.

Danny ran down another aisle. He turned the corner.

There was his mother! His mom was at the end of the aisle, looking at items on the shelf.

Then, Danny saw something else.

The giant dinosaur! It was sneaking up behind his mother!

Oh, no!

Chapter Six

Danny was terrified.

"Mom!" he shouted. "Look out!"

But by then, it was already too late.

The dinosaur took a step forward. He moved closer to

Danny's mother.

His mouth was open.

His teeth showed.

Danny knew he had to do something.

He looked around.

On the shelf, he spotted a large red plastic ball. He grabbed it.

Holding it in one hand, he drew the ball back. He aimed for the dinosaur. Then, he threw the plastic ball as hard as he could.

The red ball sailed through the air. It bounced off the dinosaur's nose!

Then, something amazing happened.

The dinosaur vanished! It disappeared and was gone.

But the red plastic ball hit Danny's mother in the back of her head! The ball bounced to the floor.

Danny's mother turned. She looked at the red plastic ball at her feet.

She looked up and saw Danny.

"Danny," she said sharply. "You know better than to throw things in the store."

"But there was a giant dinosaur attacking you!" Danny said. "I saved your life!"

Danny's mother shook her head. She held out her hand.

"Come on," she said. "It's time to check out and go home."

Danny took his mother's hand. He looked around for the dinosaur. It was gone.

He and his mother walked to the front of the store. Danny looked at the many items on the shelves. At the checkout counter, his mother paid for her things, and they left.

Danny wondered what would happen the next time he visited the dollar store.

The End

Check out some of these chilling,

American Chillers:

#1: The Michigan Mega-Monsters
#2: Ogres of Ohio
#3: Florida Fog Phantoms
#4: New York Ninjas
#5: Terrible Tractors of Texas
#6: Invisible Iguanas of Illinois
#7: Wisconsin Werewolves
#8: Minnesota Mall Mannequins
#9: Iron Insects Invade Indiana
#10: Missouri Madhouse
#11: Poisonous Pythons Paralyze Pennsylvania
#12: Dangerous Dolls of Delaware
#13: Virtual Vampires of Vermont
#14: Creepy Condors of California
#15: Nebraska Nightcrawlers
#16: Alien Androids Assault Arizona
#17: South Carolina Sea Creatures
#18: Washington Wax Museum
#19: North Dakota Night Dragons
#20: Mutant Mammoths of Montana
#21: Terrifying Toys of Tennessee
#22: Nuclear Jellyfish of New Jersey
#23: Wicked Velociraptors of West Virginia
#24: Haunting in New Hampshire
#25: Mississippi Megalodon
#26: Oklahoma Outbreak
#27: Kentucky Komodo Dragons
#28: Curse of the Connecticut Coyotes
#29: Oregon Oceanauts
#30: Vicious Vacuums of Virginia
#31: The Nevada Nightmare Novel
#32: Idaho Ice Beast
#33: Monster Mosquitoes of Maine
#34: Savage Dinosaurs of South Dakota
#35: Maniac Martians Marooned in Massachusetts
#36: Carnivorous Crickets of Colorado
#37: The Underground Undead of Utah
#38: The Wicked Waterpark of Wyoming
#39: Angry Army Ants Ambush Alabama
#40: Incredible Ivy of Iowa
#41: North Carolina Night Creatures
#42: Arctic Anacondas of Alaska
#43: Robotic Rodents Ravage Rhode Island

great books by Johnathan Rand!

Michigan Chillers:

#1: Mayhem on Mackinac Island
#2: Terror Stalks Traverse City
#3: Poltergeists of Petoskey
#4: Aliens Attack Alpena
#5: Gargoyles of Gaylord
#6: Strange Spirits of St. Ignace
#7: Kreepy Klowns of Kalamazoo
#8: Dinosaurs Destroy Detroit
#9: Sinister Spiders of Saginaw
#10: Mackinaw City Mummies
#11: Great Lakes Ghost Ship
#12: AuSable Alligators
#13: Gruesome Ghouls of Grand Rapids
#14: Bionic Bats of Bay City
#15: Calumet Copper Creatures
#16: Catastrophe in Caseville
#17: A Ghostly Haunting in Grand Haven
#18: Sault Ste. Marie Sea Monsters
#19: Drummond Island Dogman
#20: Lair of the Lansing Leprechauns

Freddie Fernortner, Fearless First Grader:

#1: The Fantastic Flying Bicycle
#2: The Super-Scary Night Thingy
#3: A Haunting We Will Go
#4: Freddie's Dog Walking Service
#5: The Big Box Fort
#6: Mr. Chewy's Big Adventure
#7: The Magical Wading Pool
#8: Chipper's Crazy Carnival
#9: Attack of the Dust Bunnies
from Outer Space!
#10: The Pond Monster
#11: Tadpole Trouble
#12: Frankenfreddie
#13: Day of the Dinosaurs

American Chillers Double Thrillers:

Vampire Nation &
Attack of the Monster Venus Melon

Dollar $tore Danny:

#1: The Dangerous Dinosaur
#2: The Salt Shaker Spaceship
#3: The Crazy Crayons

Adventure Club series:

#1: Ghost in the Graveyard
#2: Ghost in the Grand
#3: The Haunted Schoolhouse

For Teens:

PANDEMIA: A novel of the
bird flu and the end of the world
(written with Christopher Knight)

All AudioCraft Publishing, Inc. books are proudly printed, bound, and manufactured in the United States of America, utilizing American resources, labor, and materials.

USA